USBORNE SPOTTER'S GUIDES

SEASHORE STICKER BOOK

Edited by Lisa Miles
Designed by Fiona Johnson and Karen Webb

Cover illustration by Ian Jackson
Line illustrations by Guy Smith

Stickers illustrated by John Barber, Trevor Boyer, Hilary Burn, Alan Harris, Annabel Milne and Peter Stebbing

How to use this book

There are over a hundred different plants and animals described in this book. Using the descriptions and the line drawings, try to find the right sticker to go with each plant or animal. If you need help, there is a list at the end of the book that tells you which stickers go with which plant or animal. You can also use this book as a spotter's handbook to make a note of which seashore plants and animals you have seen.

Some of the descriptions in the book refer to different areas on the seashore. This diagram shows where they are.

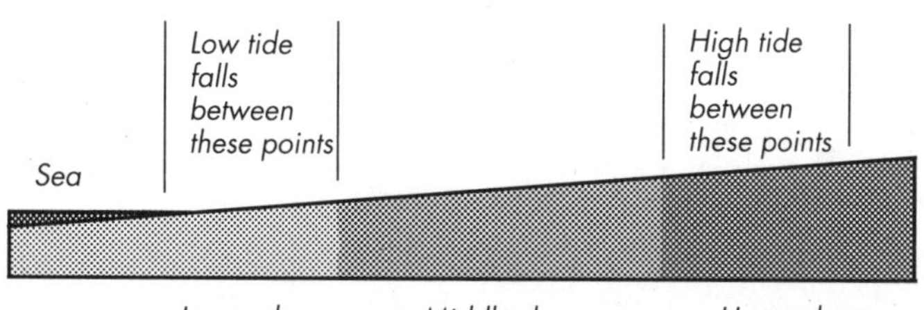

SHELLS

Empty shells once belonged to living creatures, called mollusks. Mollusks have soft bodies and grow shells around them to protect them. Some live on the seashore. Others live in the sea, but you might find their empty shells washed up on the shore.

Common Whelk

Dog Whelk

Length: 3cm (1.25in)

Whelks are gastropods – they have a muscular foot attached to them inside their shell that clings to rocks or seaweed. Dog Whelks are common in the Eastern Atlantic. Those that feed on barnacles become white, while those that feed on mussels (see page 4) become black.

DATE	
PLACE	

Dog Whelk

Blue-rayed Limpet

Common Limpet

Length: 7cm (2.75in)

Limpets are gastropods, like whelks. They clamp themselves to rocks with their muscular foot. During the night, Common Limpets feed on seaweed at low tide. They are often seen on rocky shores.

DATE	
PLACE	

Common Limpet

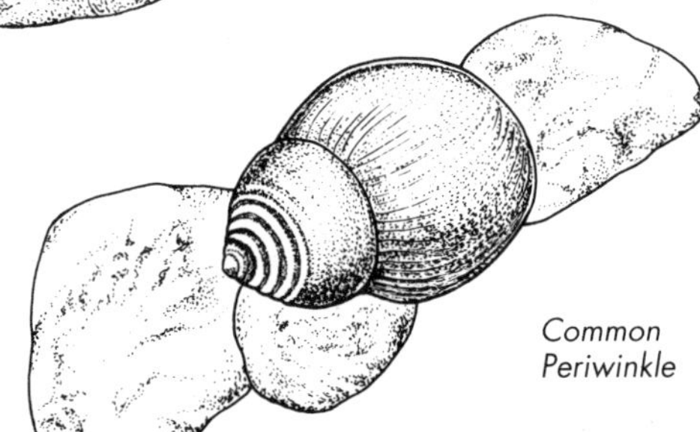

Common Periwinkle

Common Whelk

Length: 8cm (3in)

The Common Whelk is very commonly seen on both rocky and sandy beaches. It is usually found on the lower shore, on beaches of the Eastern Atlantic.

DATE	
PLACE	

Blue-rayed Limpet

Length: 1.5cm (0.5in)

Like other limpets, the Blue-rayed Limpet feeds on seaweed. On a young limpet, the rays of blue dots on its shell are bright. On an old one, they are faded. You can see them on brown seaweeds of the Eastern Atlantic.

DATE	
PLACE	

Common Periwinkle

Length: 2.5cm (1in)

Look for the Common Periwinkle close to the sea on all kinds of shores. It feeds on seaweed.

DATE	
PLACE	

Flat Periwinkle

Flat Periwinkle

Length: 1cm (0.5in)

Flat Periwinkles feed on wrack seaweeds (see page 22). They are fairly common and look like bladders on seaweed. They can be yellow, orange, brown or striped.

DATE	
PLACE	

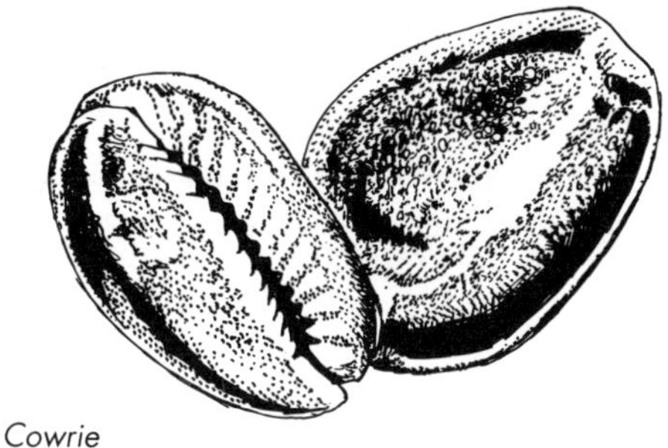

Cowrie Shell

Cowrie Shell

Length: 1.2cm (0.75in)

There are several kinds of Cowrie Shells. A small type is shown here. Look for these under stones and crevices. Giant Cowrie Shells are found on the shores of North America.

DATE	
PLACE	

Top Shell

Top Shell

Length: 2.5cm (1in)

The Top Shell lives on rocks and under stones. It can be yellow or pink, with red stripes.

DATE	
PLACE	

Moon Snail

Moon Snail

Length: 4cm (1.5in)

This creature preys on other mollusks by drilling a neat hole in shells and eating the flesh inside. It is found on sandy shores.

DATE	
PLACE	

Duck Foot Shell

Length: 5.5cm (2.25in)

This gets its name from its distinctive shape. The edges of the shell are shaped like a webbed foot. It is not common, but you may see them on the shore.

DATE	
PLACE	

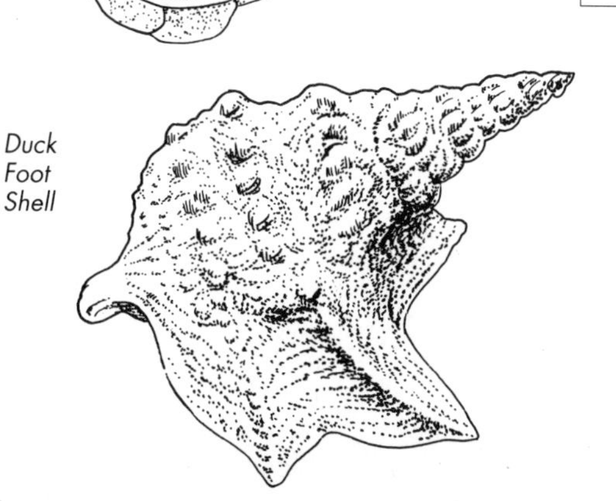

Duck Foot Shell

TWO-SHELLED CREATURES

Some mollusks (see page 2) are bivalves. This means that they have two shells hinged together with muscles. All the shells on this page are bivalves.

Common Mussel

Length: 1-10cm (0.5-4in)

Common Mussels are blue or brown and found on rocky shores and in estuaries. They attach themselves to rocks by thin threads. People collect this kind of mussel to eat.

DATE	
PLACE	

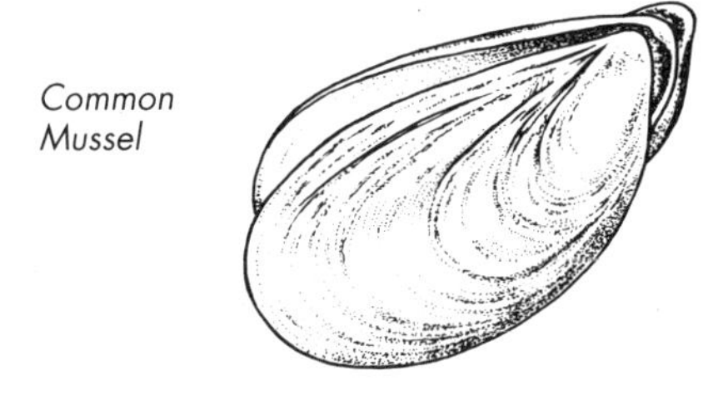

Common Mussel

Razor Shell

Length: 15cm (6in)

Razor Shells look like old-fashioned razor blades. The creature inside lives buried in sand or mud, often as deep as 1m (3.25ft). The two shells are hinged at one end.

DATE	
PLACE	

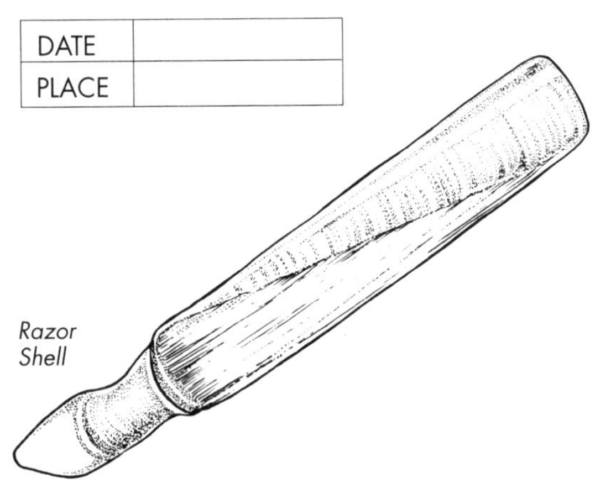

Razor Shell

Virginia Oyster

Width: 6cm (2.25in)

The Virginia Oyster sticks firmly to rocks. The shell often follows the shape of the rock. It is found on the middle shore.

DATE	
PLACE	

Virginia Oyster

Heart Cockle

Width: 9.5cm (3.75in)

If you look at the side of this shell, you will see a heart shape, which is how it got its name. It lives in muddy sand below the low tide level, but may be washed ashore.

DATE	
PLACE	

Heart Cockle

Scallop

Width: up to 9cm (3.5in)

Scallops move around by clapping their two shells together, forcing water out behind them to jet themselves along. There are several hundred species of scallops.

DATE	
PLACE	

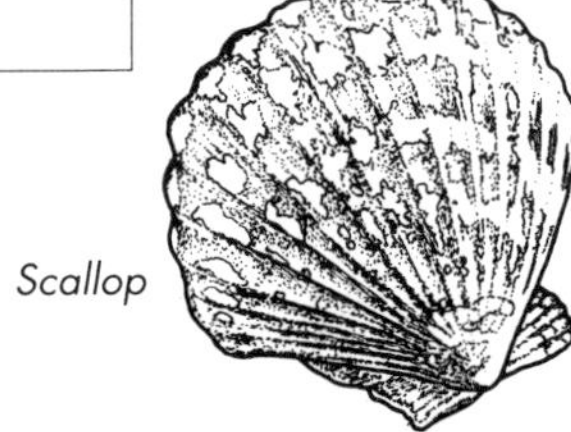

Scallop

SOFT-BODIED CREATURES

Unlike the creatures on the opposite page, some mollusks have no shells to protect their outsides. All the soft-bodied creatures on this page are mollusks.

Plumed Sea Slug

Length: 7cm (3in)

This animal is common on rocky shores on the middle shore, under stones. It feeds on sea anemones (see page 20).

DATE	
PLACE	

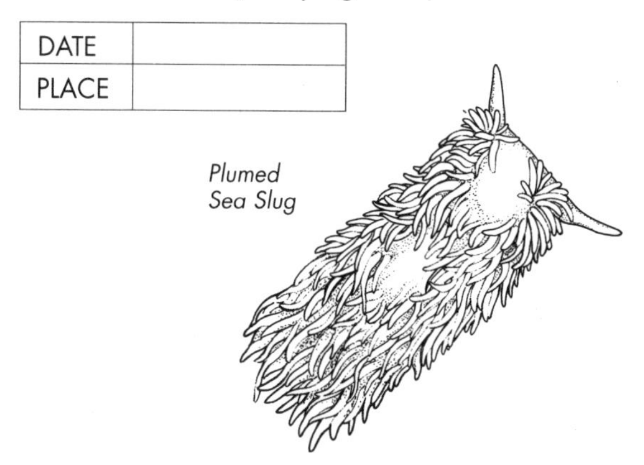

Plumed Sea Slug

Common Octopus

Length: 20cm (8in), not including tentacles

This octopus lives among rocks and stones. It is occasionally found on the extreme lower shore. The tide has to be a long way out for you to see it.

DATE	
PLACE	

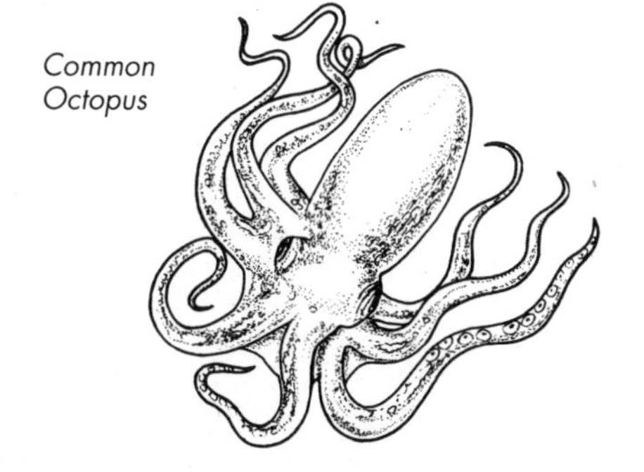

Common Octopus

Limacia clavigera

Length: 2cm (0.75in)

This mollusk lives in shallow water. Its body is usually white with red-tipped fronds along its back. Its bright markings warn predators that it tastes nasty.

DATE	
PLACE	

Limacia clavigera

Common Cuttlefish

Length: 30cm (12in)

The cuttlefish has a large soft body supported by a thick shell inside it. The shell is called a cuttlebone. Cuttlebones are often washed ashore.

DATE	
PLACE	

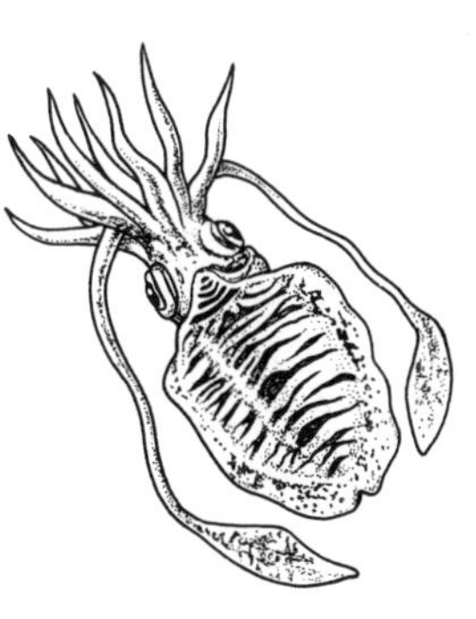

Common Cuttlefish

Common Squid

Length: up to 60cm (24in)

Squid are rarely found near the shore. They have ten arms and large, soft bodies supported by an inside shell, called a pen. You may often see pens washed ashore.

DATE	
PLACE	

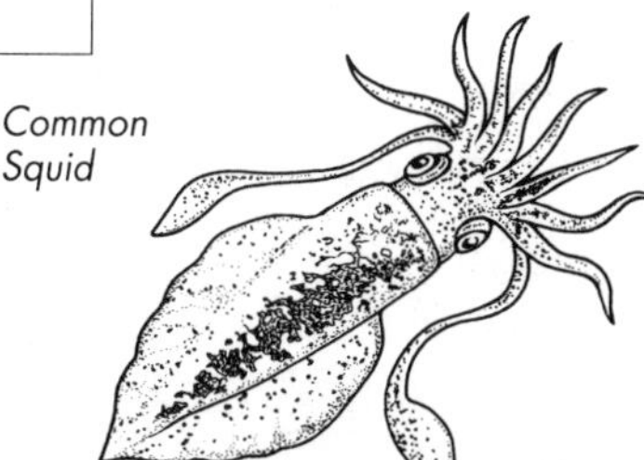

Common Squid

CRABS AND THEIR RELATIVES

These creatures all belong to the crustacean family. Their soft bodies are protected by a hard shell.

Common Hermit Crab

Length: 10cm (4in)

The Hermit Crab has no shell of its own to protect its body, so it finds an empty shell to live in. When it outgrows the shell, it finds a new one. It can be found in rock pools.

DATE	
PLACE	

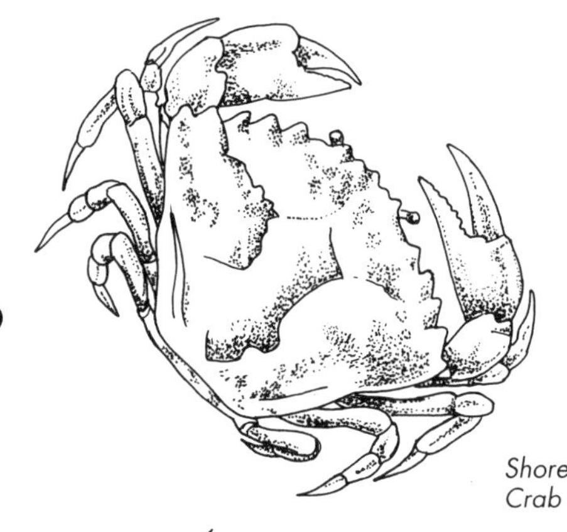

Shore Crab

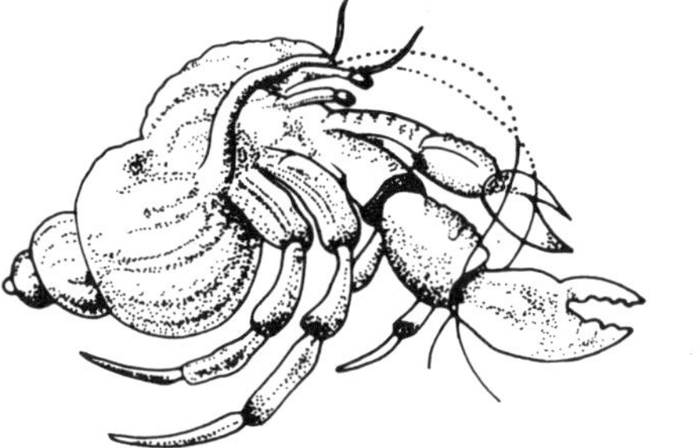

Common Hermit Crab

Shore Crab

Length: 4cm (1.5in)

The Shore Crab has a smooth, broad shell. Young ones often have pretty markings. It is common on both sandy and rocky shores. When the tide is out, it hides from seabirds in the mud.

DATE	
PLACE	

Common Lobster

Length: up to 45cm (18in)

Small Common Lobsters are sometimes found in rock pools on the lower shore. Most lobsters, though, crawl along the seabed in deep waters.

Common Lobster

DATE	
PLACE	

Blue Swimming Crab

Length: 8cm (3in)

This crab can be found on the lower shore. It has a hairy shell and its back legs are flattened for swimming.

DATE	
PLACE	

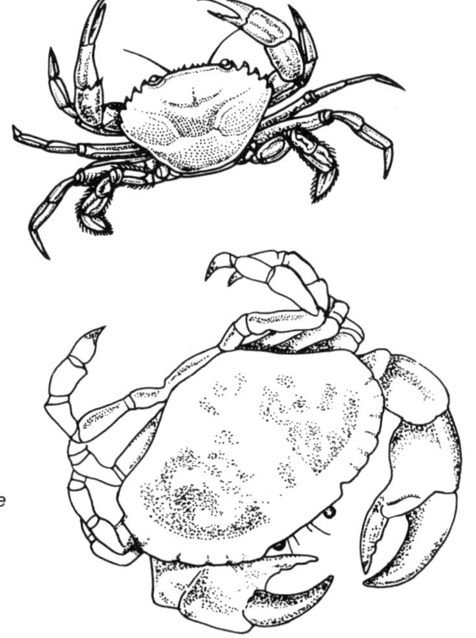

Blue Swimming Crab

Edible Rock Crab

Edible Rock Crab

Length: up to 11.5cm (4.5in)

Large Edible Rock Crabs live in deep water, but you can see small ones in rock pools, under rocks or buried under sand on the lower shore. As you can guess from their name, these crabs can be eaten.

DATE	
PLACE	

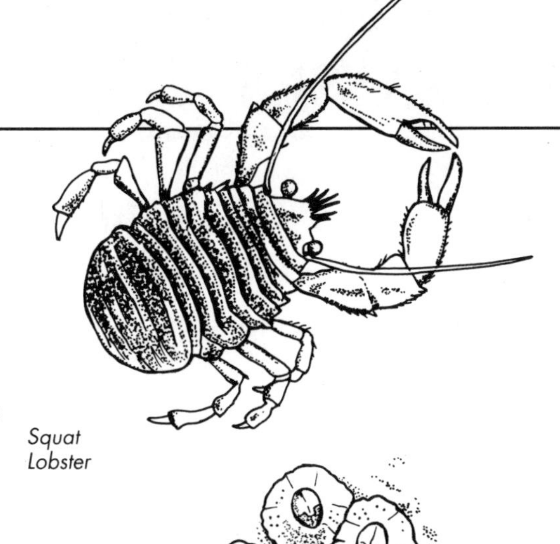

Squat Lobster

Squat Lobster

Length: 45cm (18in)

This is not a true lobster, but a relative. It is found under rocks and stones on the lower shore. Its first pair of walking legs have very long pincers.

DATE	
PLACE	

Acorn Barnacle

Acorn Barnacle

Length: 1.5cm (0.5in)

Barnacles stick to rocks and build a hard shell around themselves, like a wall. They are a very common sight on rocks. The Acorn Barnacle has a diamond-shaped opening.

DATE	
PLACE	

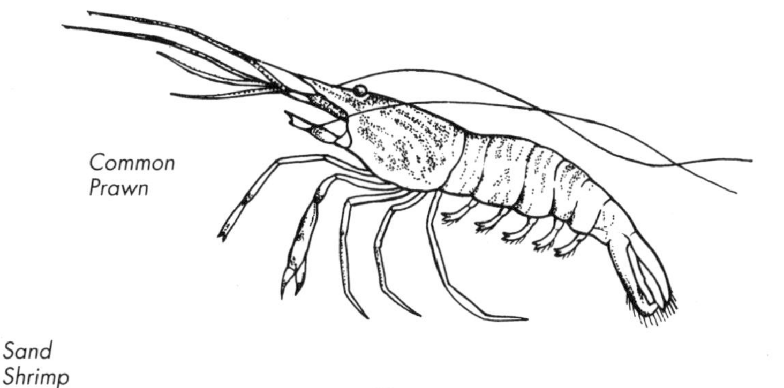

Common Prawn

Common Prawn

Length: 6.5cm (2.5in)

This creature is common in shallow water and you can sometimes find it in rock pools. Like all prawns and shrimps, its feelers are longer than its body.

DATE	
PLACE	

Sand Shrimp

Sand Shrimp

Length: 5cm (2in)

This shrimp is common in sandy estuaries. It has broad, flattened claws on its front legs. People catch shrimps and prawns to eat.

DATE	
PLACE	

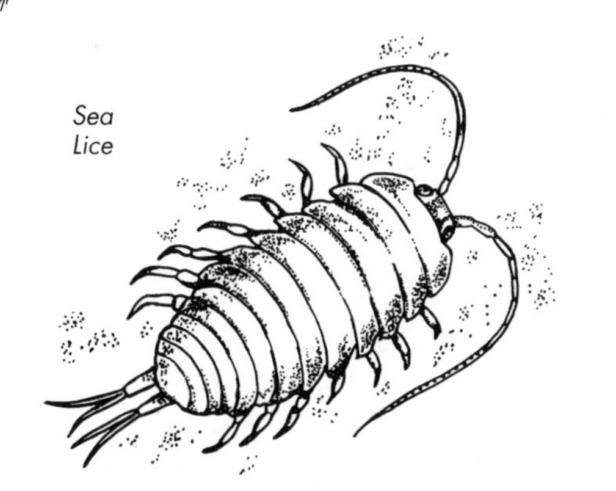

Sea Lice

Sea Lice

Length: 2.5cm (1in)

For this animal, look in breakwaters and on rocks above the high tide level on the upper shore. It is nocturnal – it comes out at night to feed.

DATE	
PLACE	

FLOWERS AND GRASSES

Seashore plants have to defend themselves against the salt spray and strong sea winds. To do this, they often grow close to the ground and have deep, tough roots.

Sea Holly

Height: 50cm (20in)

This prickly plant has clusters of tiny flowers, which attract butterflies. Its leaves turn white in winter. It is found on sand and shingle beaches.

Sea Holly

DATE	
PLACE	

Sea Kale

Height: 1m (3.25ft)

Sea Kale grows in clumps on shingle. It has broad, fleshy leaves with crinkly edges. It flowers in summer.

Sea Kale

DATE	
PLACE	

Sea Campion

Height: 20cm (8in)

Common on cliffs and shingle beaches, Sea Campion spreads out to form soft cushions. It flowers in midsummer.

Sea Campion

DATE	
PLACE	

Sea Bindweed

Sea Bindweed

Height: 10cm (4in)

This trailing plant grows along the ground and binds the sand together. It has thick, shiny leaves and can be seen on sandy beaches, and sometimes on shingle. It flowers from mid to late summer.

DATE	
PLACE	

Yellow Horned Poppy

Yellow Horned Poppy

Height: 1m (3.25ft)

The Yellow Horned Poppy gets its name from its long seed pods. It flowers from mid to late summer and is found on shingle beaches in the Eastern Atlantic.

DATE	
PLACE	

Sea Aster

Sea Aster

Height: 1m (3.25ft)

The Sea Aster is found in salt marshes. Salt marsh plants are unusual, because they are regularly covered by the tide. This one flowers in late summer with mauve or white petals.

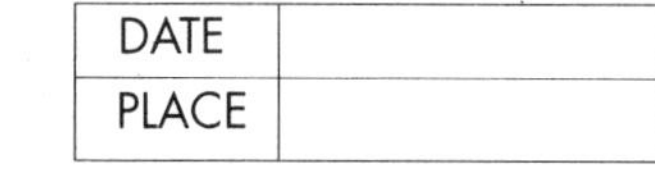

DATE	
PLACE	

Bird's Foot Trefoil

Height: 10cm (4in)

The flowers on this plant are bright yellow and streaked with red. The seed pods split and curl when they are ripe, to release the seeds. It is found on grassy banks and cliffs.

DATE	
PLACE	

Thrift

Height: 15cm (6in)

This plant (also called Sea Pink) grows in thick cushiony tufts on rocky beaches or cliffs. It is particularly good at surviving salty spray. Look for the flowers between spring and late summer.

DATE	
PLACE	

Sea Couch Grass

Sea Couch Grass

Height: 40cm (16in)

Sea Couch Grass has long roots and binds sand together. Ridges of sand build up around it, just above the high tide level.

DATE	
PLACE	

Marram Grass

Marram Grass

Height: 1.2m (4ft)

This plant is very common on sand dunes. Its long roots and leaves trap sand and stop it from being blown away. It flowers in mid-summer.

DATE	
PLACE	

Sea Lavender

Height: 40cm (16in)

This is a tough plant, that has leaves in a clump near the ground. It flowers from mid-summer.

DATE	
PLACE	

Sea Lavender

California Poppy

Height: 40cm (16in)

The California Poppy has delicate, saucer-shaped flowers that close in dull weather. It flowers in the summer.

DATE	
PLACE	

California Poppy

CLIFF BIRDS

Many seabirds live in large groups, called colonies, on rocky cliffs. Each different species, or type, of bird builds its nest at a different height. Birds gather on cliffs during the breeding season in spring and early summer. The rest of the year, the cliffs are deserted as the birds migrate or feed out at sea.

Shag

Shag

Length: 75cm (29.5in)

The crest on top of the Shag's head is only seen in the breeding season, in the spring. It is found on Eastern Atlantic shores.

DATE	
PLACE	

Cormorant

Cormorant

Length: 90cm (36in)

This bird is seen mainly near the sea, but can sometimes be seen inland on lakes and reservoirs. Its wings are not waterproof, so you may see it holding them out to dry.

DATE	
PLACE	

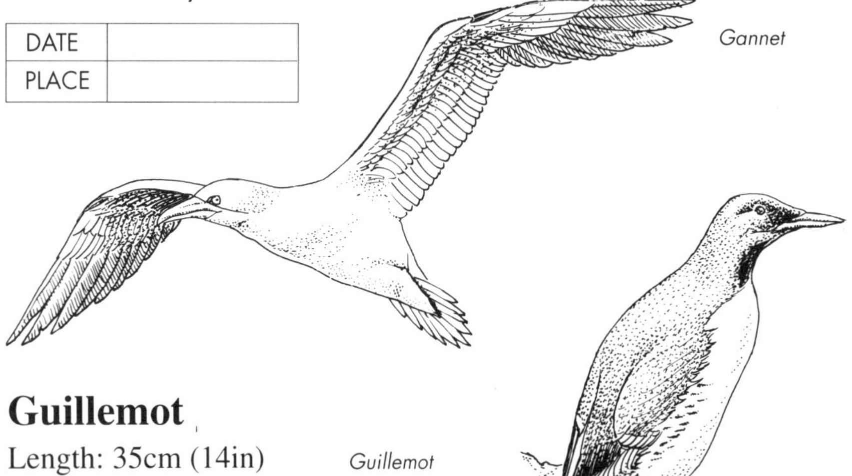

Gannet

Gannet

Length: 90cm (36in)

Gannets can be seen out at sea, where they dive headfirst from a great height into the water to catch fish. They nest on rocky coasts, building messy nests around 1m (3.25ft) apart.

DATE	
PLACE	

Guillemot

Guillemot

Length: 35cm (14in)

The Guillemot perches on bare ledges without a nest. It lays a single egg straight onto the cliff ledge. The eggs are pear-shaped, so that they spin when knocked, so that they don't roll off.

DATE	
PLACE	

Razorbill

Razorbill

Length: 40cm (16in)

The Razorbill's flat-sided beak makes it easy to distinguish from other birds. It likes to nest in cavities in the cliffs, though some will nest on ledges with Guillemots.

DATE	
PLACE	

Herring Gull

Length: 60cm (24in)

As well as on cliffs, the Herring Gull sometimes nests on the ground and even on buildings. It is noisy and is often seen inland, as well as on coasts, where it scavenges for food.

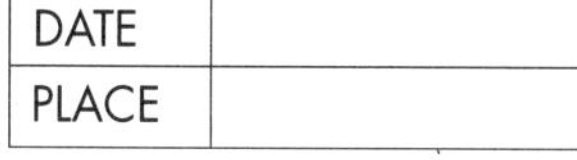

DATE	
PLACE	

Great Black-backed Gull

Length: 70cm (27.5in)

This is a very large gull, with a wingspan of 1.5m (5ft). It is very aggressive and sometimes kills and eats other seabirds. It is usually seen alone or in small numbers.

DATE	
PLACE	

Fulmar

Length: 45cm (17.5in)

The Fulmar looks like a gull, except it is fatter and fluffier. It glides along on stiff wings, and flies with short wing beats. It spends most of its time out at sea, off Eastern Atlantic shores.

DATE	
PLACE	

Fulmar

Kittiwake

Kittiwake

Length: 45cm (17.5in)

This bird is a small gull and spends most of its time out at sea, where it can be seen following ships. When breeding, it makes a nest of green seaweed stuck to the cliff with mud.

DATE	
PLACE	

Puffin

Length: 30cm (12in)

The Puffin lives far out to sea, except in the breeding season. It nests in colonies in burrows on turfy cliff tops and islands. It has a bright bill in the summer.

Puffin

DATE	
PLACE	

SHORE BIRDS

Salt marshes and muddy shores are good places to see ducks and geese. Sandy beaches are good places to spot gulls and terns. Long-legged waders can be seen on all kinds of shores. These birds dig in sand to find things to eat.

Common Tern

Length: 34cm (13.5in)

The Common Tern nests in groups on beaches and sand dunes. It has long wings and long tail feathers that can easily be seen when it is flying. It dives to catch small fish.

DATE	
PLACE	

Curlew

Length: 48-64cm (19-25in)

The Curlew has a long curved beak that is an unmistakable shape. It uses its beak to probe deep down in the sand for creatures such as lugworms. In spring the Curlew breeds in open grasslands, but spends winter by the shore.

DATE	
PLACE	

Shelduck

Length: 60cm (24in)

Flocks of Shelducks are a common sight in Europe. They often nest in old rabbit holes in the sand dunes. They feed on small mollusks in shallow water.

DATE	
PLACE	

Black-headed Gull

Length: 38cm (15in)

This is a very common gull, which is seen as often inland as it is on the coast. It nests in colonies on marshes, dunes and in shingle. Its head is dark only during the summer months. It has a red beak and legs.

DATE	
PLACE	

Ringed Plover

Length: 20cm (8in)

This bird is seen on sandy and shingle shores, and also near estuaries in the winter. It usually nests on shingle on the coast. It also nests inland, though rarely.

DATE	
PLACE	

1
2
3
4
5
6
7
8
9
10
1
12
13

MAMMALS

All these animals live on the shore or in the water. Although some live or spend a long time in the water, they are all mammals – they need air to breathe.

California Sea Lion

California Sea Lion

Length: 2.3m (7.5ft)

This animal lives off the shores of the Pacific coast of North America. It swims by moving its forearms. When its coat is dry, it is light fawn.

DATE	
PLACE	

Harbor Seal

Length: 1.8m (6ft)

The skin tone of this seal varies, but adults are always spotty. It lives in herds on sandbanks, in estuaries. It is a fast swimmer and can dive down under the water for up to 20 or 30 minutes.

Harbor Seal

DATE	
PLACE	

Common Porpoise

Length: 1.8m (6ft)

This animal is a small whale that has teeth and a blunt nose. It often swims near the coast in schools. It eats squid, herring and other small fish.

DATE	
PLACE	

Common Porpoise

Common Dolphin

Length: 2.4m (8ft)

The Common Dolphin has a long slim body and a narrow nose, called a beak. It is a fast swimmer. It swims in large groups, called schools, and is very playful, often jumping right out of the water.

DATE	
PLACE	

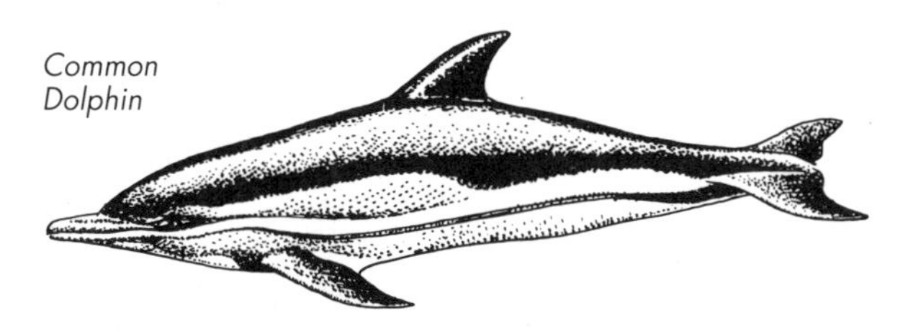

Common Dolphin

Gray Seal

Length: 2.9m (9.5ft)

The Gray Seal lives in small herds on rocky shores. It rests on land at low tide and at sunset, but it also sleeps in the water.

DATE	
PLACE	

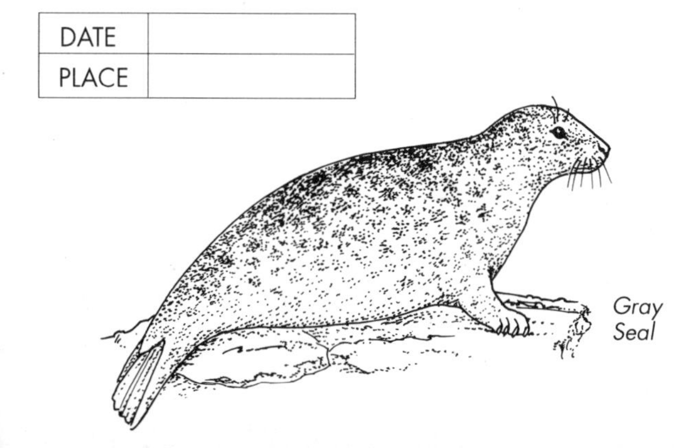

Gray Seal

FISHES

Around the seashore, there are many kinds of fishes. Some burrow into the sand in shallow water and come out again at high tide to look for food. Others live in rocky areas, pools, under stones or among seaweed.

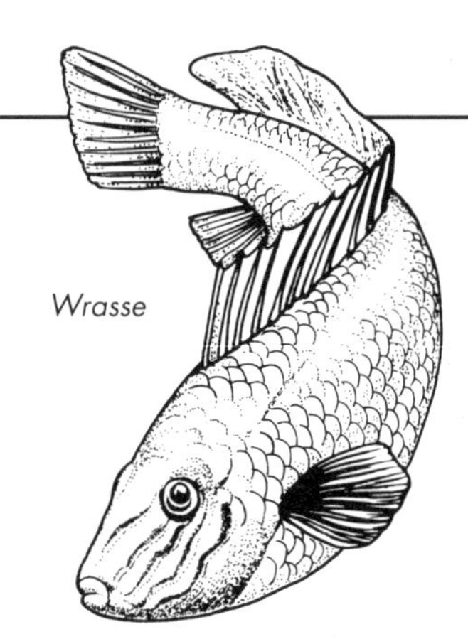

Wrasse

Wrasse

Length: 25cm (10in)

The Wrasse begins life as a female and then becomes male with age. It eats animals with shells, which it crushes with its strong teeth. It lives in weedy pools.

DATE	
PLACE	

Gunnels

Length: 25cm (10in)

Gunnels live in cool waters and slide their slender bodies between the rocks where they live. They also live under seaweed and under stones, on all kinds of shores.

Gunnels

DATE	
PLACE	

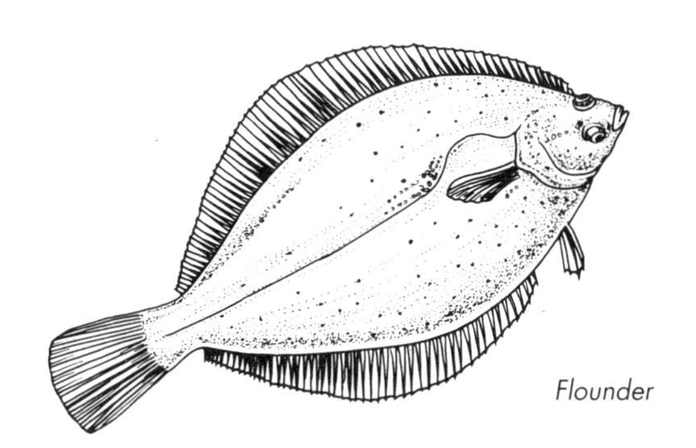

Flounder

Flounder

Length: 25cm (10in)

The Flounder is very common on sandy or muddy bottoms. You can often see it in shallow water. It eats small crustaceans.

DATE	
PLACE	

Pipefish

Length: 45cm (18in)

The Pipefish is common on muddy or sandy bottoms. It eats young fishes and tiny crustaceans. It can be very hard to see, because it camouflages itself among seaweed or Eel Grass (see page 23).

DATE	
PLACE	

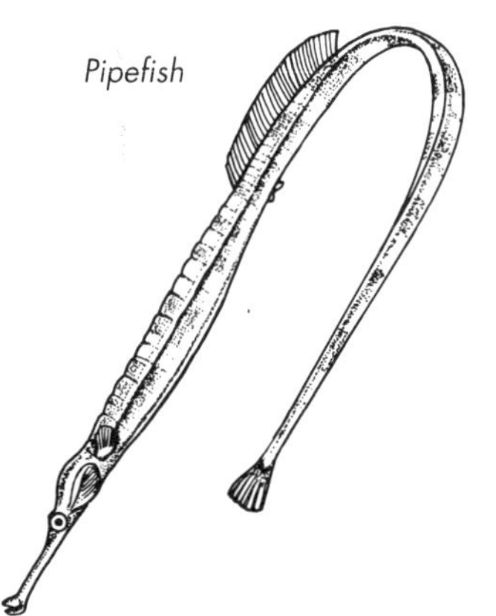

Pipefish

Sand Eel

Length: 20cm (8in)

This fish lives in huge groups, called schools, close to the sea bottom in shallow water, in the Eastern Atlantic. It burrows headfirst into the sand.

DATE	
PLACE	

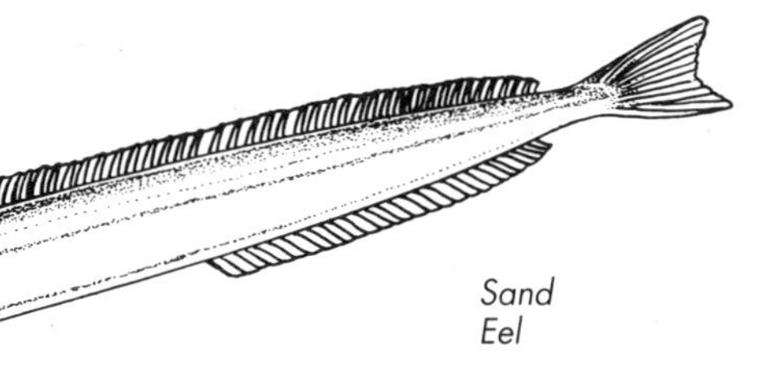

Sand Eel

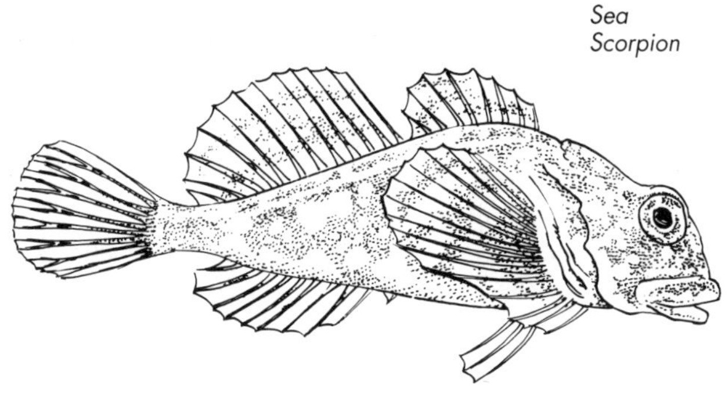
Sea Scorpion

Sea Scorpion

Length: 17cm (6.75in)

This fish is commonly seen in pools on the shore and among seaweed. It eats shrimps, small crabs and also other fishes.

DATE	
PLACE	

Rock Goby

Length: 12cm (4.75in)

The Rock Goby lives on rocky shores in rock pools and under stones. Its eyes are on the top of its head, so that it can look out for predators.

DATE	
PLACE	

Rock Goby
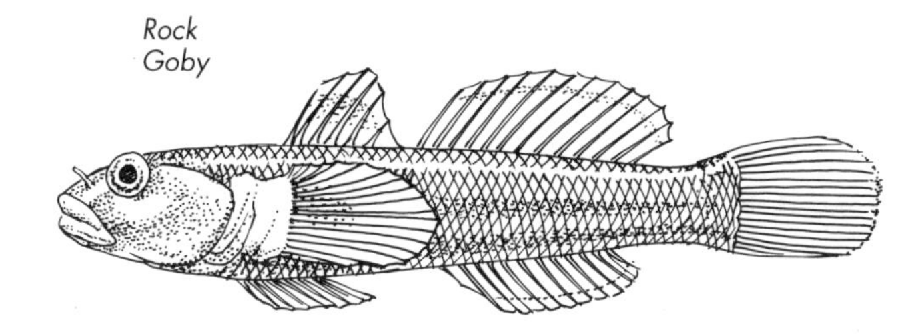

Molly Miller Blenny
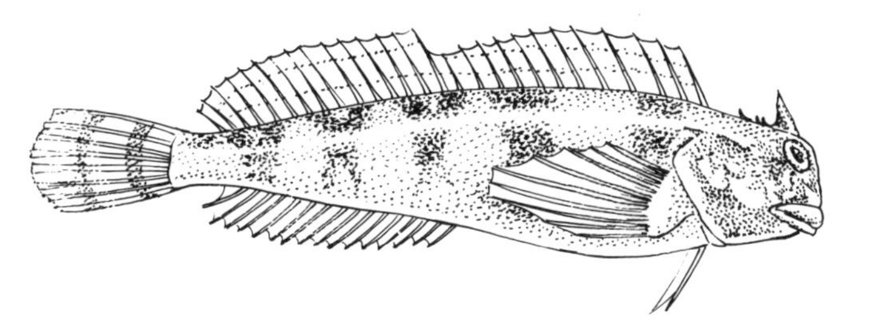

Molly Miller Blenny

Length: 8cm (3in)

This fish lives in rock pools that are almost bare of seaweed. It eats Acorn Barnacles (see page 7) that are fastened to rocks. It bites off their limbs when they come out of their shells.

DATE	
PLACE	

Clingfish

Length: 6.5cm (2.5in)

This fish lives under rocks. It clings to them with its strong sucker fin. In the summer, you may see a pair guarding their eggs.

DATE	
PLACE	

Clingfish
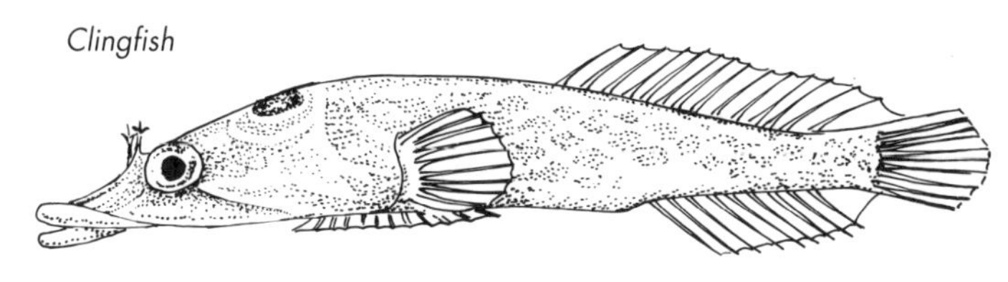

Shanny

Length: 16cm (6.25in)

The Shanny lives on both rocky and sandy shores in Europe, in pools and among seaweed. It eats small crustaceans.

DATE	
PLACE	

Shanny
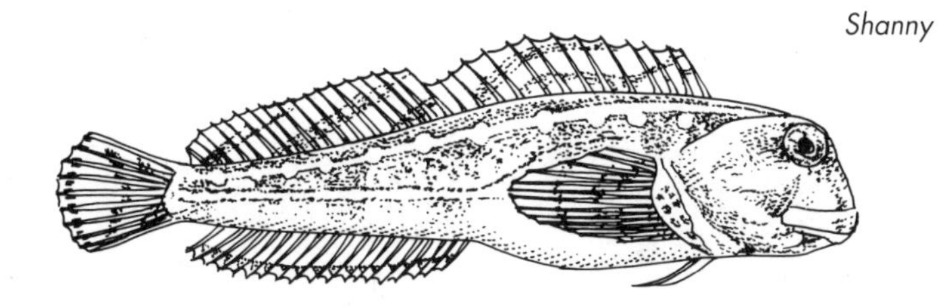

JELLYFISHES AND THEIR RELATIVES

All these creatures live in the open sea, but you may find them washed up on the shore. They push themselves along by sucking water into their bodies and then pushing it out underneath. They catch fish with their long, stinging tentacles. If you see one on the beach, don't touch.

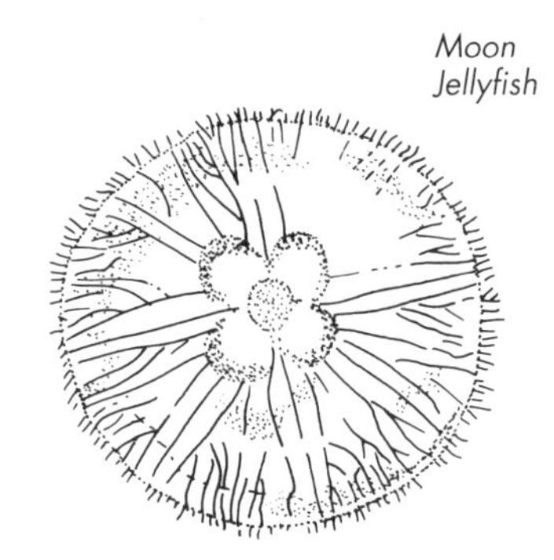

Moon Jellyfish

Width: 15cm (6in)

These jellyfish are harmless and very common. They are transparent with a purple rim and crescent shapes in the middle.

DATE	
PLACE	

Lion's Mane Jellyfish

Width: 2m (6.5ft)

The Lion's Mane Jellyfish is found only off the coasts of Europe. There are two types, blue and yellow, and they both sting.

DATE	
PLACE	

Lion's Mane Jellyfish

Stalked Jellyfish

Stalked Jellyfish

Height: 5cm (2in)

This jellyfish does not swim, but attaches itself to seaweeds on the shore. Its body has eight tufts of tentacles around the rim. It is harmless. The height shown above refers to its body only.

DATE	
PLACE	

Portuguese Man-o'-War

Width: 15cm (6in)

This is not a true jellyfish, but a close relation. It floats on the sea, but is sometimes washed ashore. All its tentacles are separate creatures, living as a colony. They can give painful stings.

DATE	
PLACE	

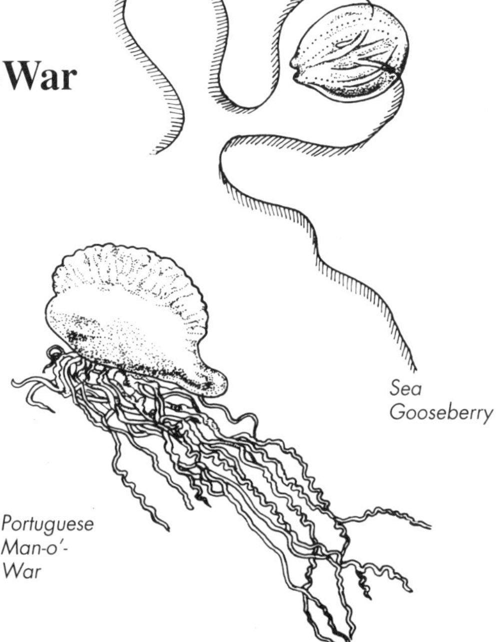

Sea Gooseberry

Width: 1cm (0.4in)

This isn't a true jellyfish either. Its transparent body is the size and shape of a gooseberry, which is how it gets its name. It catches its food in two long tentacles.

DATE	
PLACE	

WORMS

Many kinds of worms live on the seashore. Some live in tubes of sand, others burrow in the sand or move on the surface. Seashore worms are related to earthworms that live in the soil.

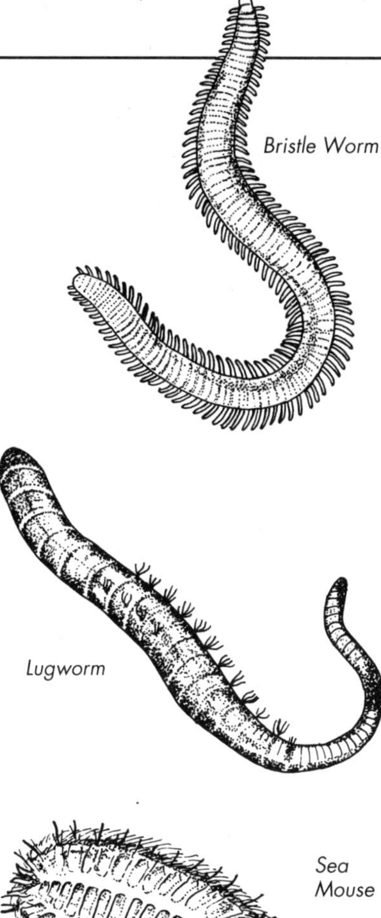

Bristle Worm

Length: 10cm (4in)

This worm burrows in sand and mud. It has bristles along each side, which help it burrow, and a red line down its back. It can be found from the middle shore to shallow water.

DATE	
PLACE	

Lugworm

Length: 15cm (6in)

Fat with a thin tail, the Lugworm lives buried in the sand. They suck in sand, digesting any edible scraps, and then pass the sand out, leaving sandcasts on the surface.

DATE	
PLACE	

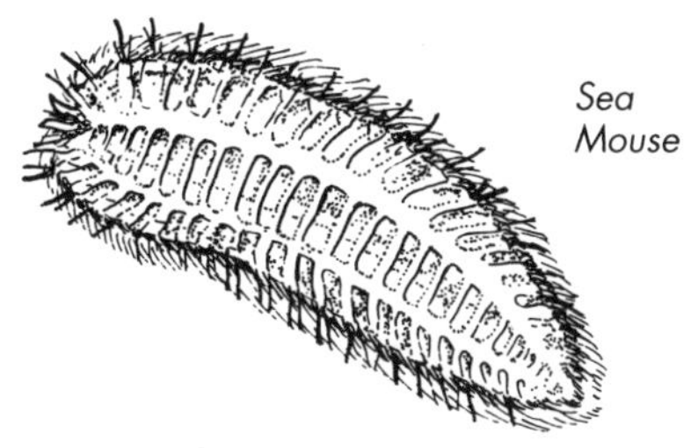

Sea Mouse

Length: 10cm (4in)

The hairy Sea Mouse is a relative of the worm family. It looks a little like a mouse if you see it swimming in the water.

DATE	
PLACE	

Limy-tube Worm

Length: 3cm (1.25in)

These worms live in hard white tubes that have a ridge along the top. Look for the tubes on rocks, stones and empty shells on the seashore.

DATE	
PLACE	

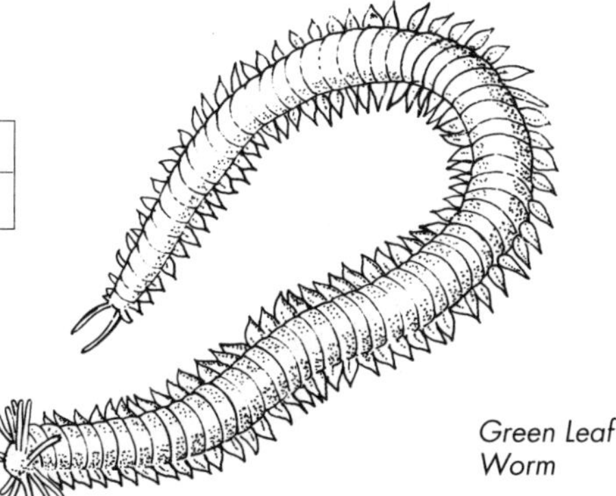

Green Leaf Worm

Length: 10cm (4in)

The Green Leaf Worm crawls among barnacles (see page 7) and under seaweed on rocks, or hides in rock crevices. It can be found from the lower shore to shallow water, on Eastern Atlantic shores.

DATE	
PLACE	

STARFISHES AND THEIR RELATIVES

These animals are all related. They have spiny skins and rows of suckers which they use for pulling themselves along and for holding onto rocks.

Common Starfish

Common Starfish

Width: 5-10cm (2-4in)

Like most starfishes, this creature has five arms. If an arm breaks off they can grow a new one. All starfishes have their mouths on the underside of their body.

DATE	
PLACE	

Common Sunstar

Common Sunstar

Width: 4-8cm (1.5-3in)

The Sunstar has up to thirteen arms. It preys on other starfishes. It is often beautifully patterned.

DATE	
PLACE	

Spiny Starfish

Spiny Starfish

Width: 8-12cm (3-5in)

Spiny Starfishes have sharp spikes to protect them against predators, such as sea snails and fish. They are found low down on the shore and in deep water, on Mediterranean and Atlantic coasts.

DATE	
PLACE	

Mediterranean Multi-armed Starfish

Width: 8-12cm (3-5in)

This starfish often has between six and eight arms, which are often of different lengths. It is only found on the shores of the Mediterranean Sea.

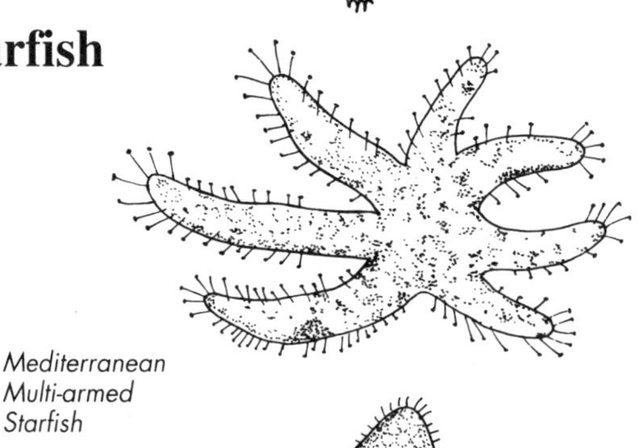

Mediterranean Multi-armed Starfish

DATE	
PLACE	

Cushion Star

Width: up to 2cm (0.75in)

The Cushion Star is a very small starfish with short arms. It likes to live in the shady parts, such as under stones.

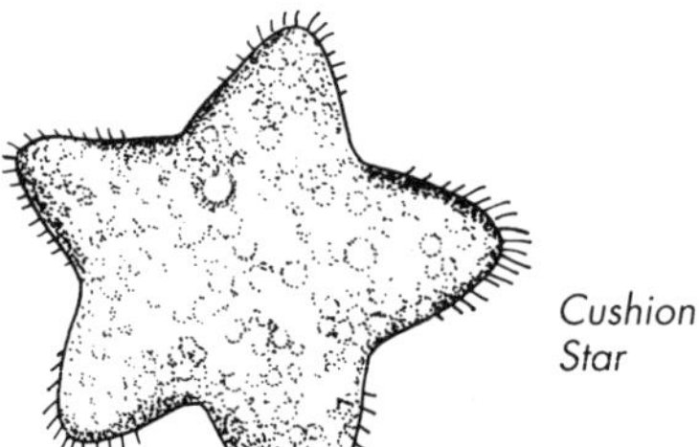

Cushion Star

DATE	
PLACE	

Common Brittle Star

Width: 3-8cm (1.25-3in)

These Brittle Stars are very common, but hard to spot because they live under stones in rock pools. They are very fragile – their long, thin arms break easily.

DATE	
PLACE	

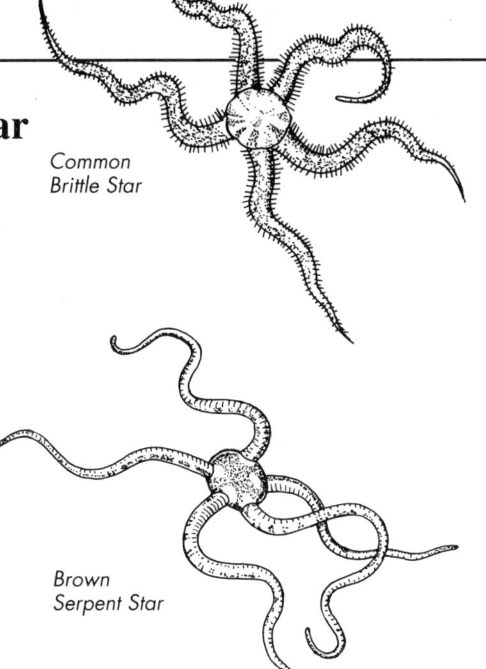

Common Brittle Star

Brown Serpent Star

Brown Serpent Star

Width: 10-15cm (4-6in)

The stripes on this Brown Serpent Star darken with age. This creature prefers to live in warm waters, such as the Mediterranean Sea.

DATE	
PLACE	

Edible Sea Urchin

Width: 15cm (6in)

Sea Urchins eat with five teeth on the base of their bodies, which they use to scrape small plants, called algae, off the rocks. The spines drop off the animal when it dies. Its empty shell is called a test. This is an Edible Sea Urchin.

Edible Sea Urchin

DATE	
PLACE	

Black Sea Urchin

Width: 6-10cm (2.25-4in)

The Black Sea Urchin has black spines. It is found on the lower shore and in deep water. It prefers warmer seas.

DATE	
PLACE	

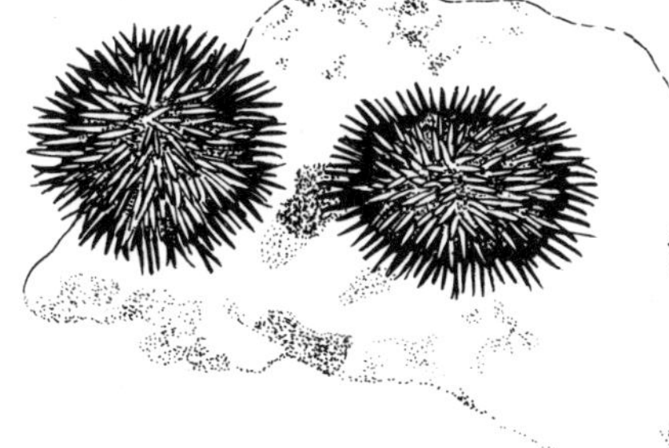

Black Sea Urchin

Sea Biscuits

Width: 5-6cm (2-2.25in)

This is a Sea Urchin that lives in the sand at the lowest tide level. It leaves a dent in the surface where it has burrowed. Empty tests may be washed ashore.

Sea Biscuits

DATE	
PLACE	

Small Purple-tipped Sea Urchin

Width: 4cm (1.5in)

This Sea Urchin lives under rocks and stones on the lower shore. Its spines have purple tips. It is more common than its relative, the Edible Sea Urchin.

DATE	
PLACE	

Small Purple-tipped Sea Urchin

SEA ANEMONES, SPONGES AND CORAL

Sea anemones, sponges and coral are animals, although they do look like delicate flowers. They are fairly common on rocks, but may be hidden.

Plumose Anemone

Height: 20cm (8in)

Plumose Anemone

The Plumose Anemone may be orange or white. It is often seen just below the water surface on pier supports.

DATE	
PLACE	

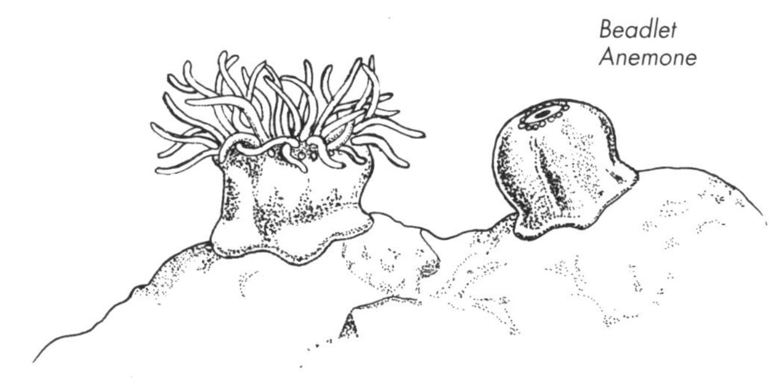

Beadlet Anemone

Beadlet Anemone

Height: 5cm (2in)

This can be red or green, with ring of blue spots below the tentacles and a thin blue line around the base. It is found only in the Eastern Atlantic.

DATE	
PLACE	

Brown Anemone

Width: 10cm (4in)

This can be brown or green. Its sticky tentacles become smaller when touched, but do not disappear. It lives on rocky shores, sometimes on Oarweed (see page 23).

DATE	
PLACE	

Brown Anemone

Painted Anemone

Height: 15cm (6in)

Painted Anemone

The Painted Anemone can be many different shades. It has a warty body, often covered with pieces of shell. This makes it hard to spot in the rock pools where it lives.

DATE	
PLACE	

Dead Men's Fingers Coral

Height: 20cm (8in)

This kind of coral lives in chunky, hand-shaped colonies. It can be white, pink or yellow. It lives offshore in cool waters, but you may see it washed up on the beach.

DATE	
PLACE	

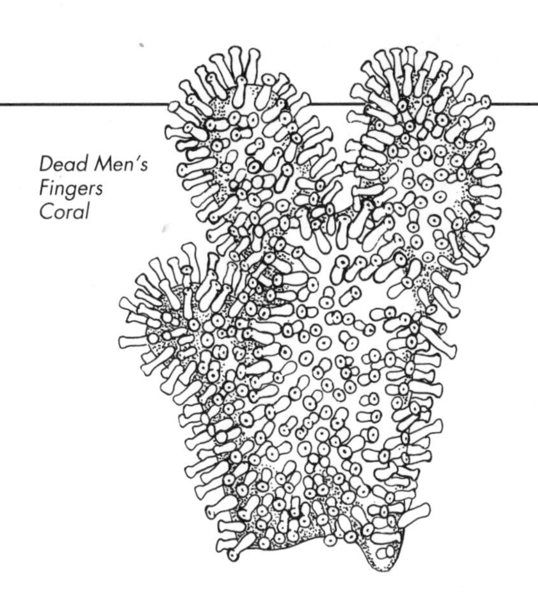

Dead Men's Fingers Coral

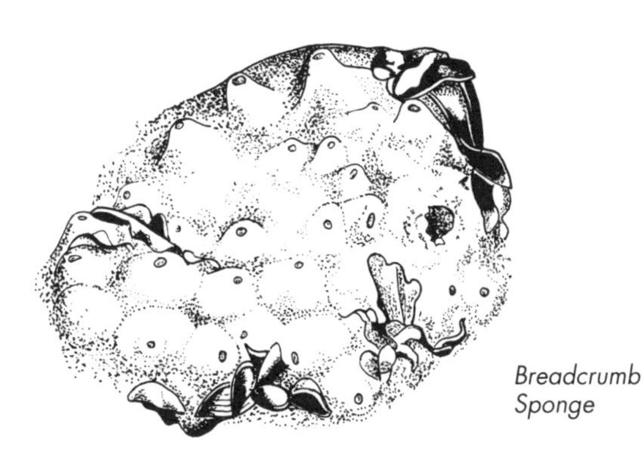

Breadcrumb Sponge

Breadcrumb Sponge

Width: 10cm (4in)

This sponge grows on rocks and seaweeds. It can be many different shapes and it varies from green to yellow. It can be found from the middle shore down to lower shore.

DATE	
PLACE	

Purse Sponge

Width: 5cm (2in)

This kind of sponge is found only in the Eastern Atlantic. It hangs down in groups under rocks, in pools and among seaweeds. It is found on the lower shore. Out of water, it collapses into a purse shape, which is how it gets its name.

DATE	
PLACE	

Purse Sponge

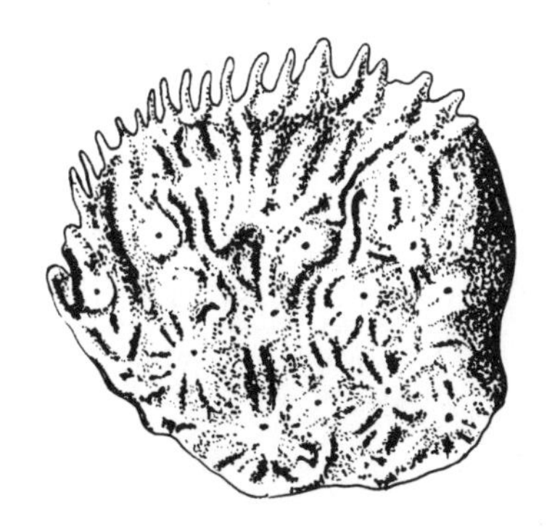

Encrusting Sponge

Encrusting Sponge

Width: 50cm (20in)

This sponge is found from the middle shore to shallow water. It forms crusts over rocks and there are many small openings all over its surface.

DATE	
PLACE	

SEAWEED

You can find many types of seaweed on the shore, especially on rocky shores. You may also see deep-water seaweed washed up on the beach. Seaweeds have a "holdfast" at the base of their stem, which holds the plant to the rock.

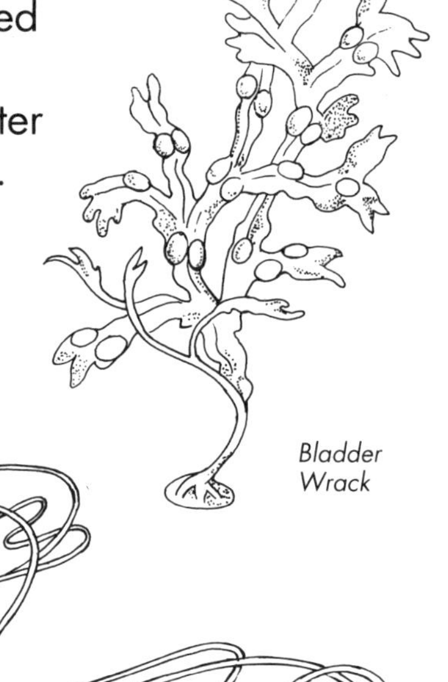

Bladder Wrack

Bladder Wrack

Height: 60cm (24in)

This seaweed gets its name from the pairs of bladders, or pockets, of air that keep it upright in the water. It has a large holdfast.

DATE	
PLACE	

Sea Twine

Length: up to 6m (19.5ft)

Sea Twine looks like long, thin cords waving in the water. It lives in shallow water and grows extremely long compared to other seaweeds.

Sea Twine

DATE	
PLACE	

Knotted Wrack

Height: 1m (3.25ft)

This seaweed grows in strap-like fronds. It can be found on sheltered rock on the middle shore. It has tufts of red seaweed growing on it.

Knotted Wrack

DATE	
PLACE	

Sea Lettuce

Height: 20cm (8in)

It is fairly common to see the wavy leaves of the Sea Lettuce on all types of shore. This seaweed grows darker with age.

DATE	
PLACE	

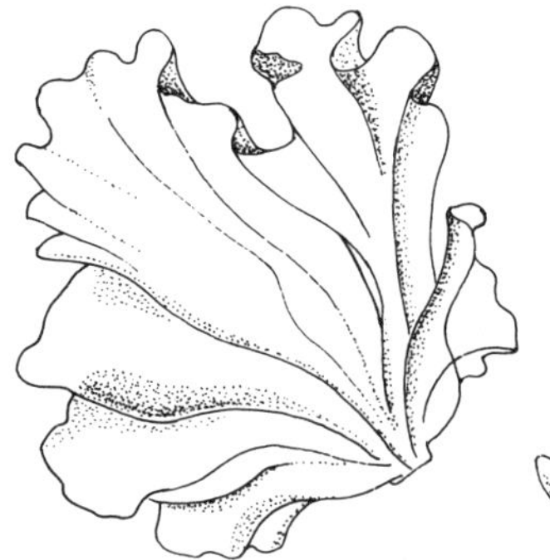

Sea Lettuce

Channel Wrack

Height: 10cm (4in)

The edges of this seaweed's fronds are curved to form channels. It is found on the upper shores of the Eastern Atlantic.

DATE	
PLACE	

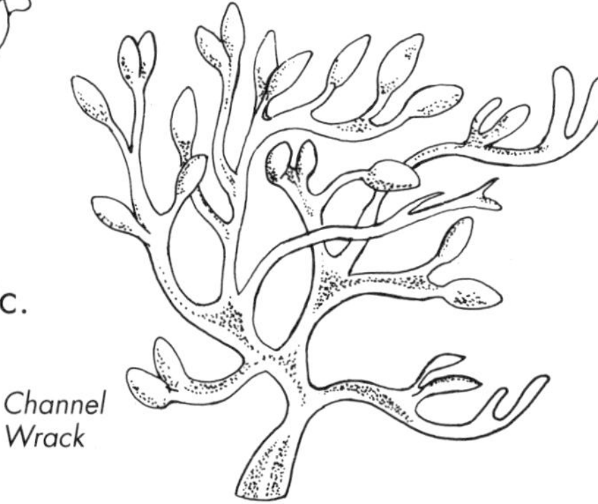

Channel Wrack

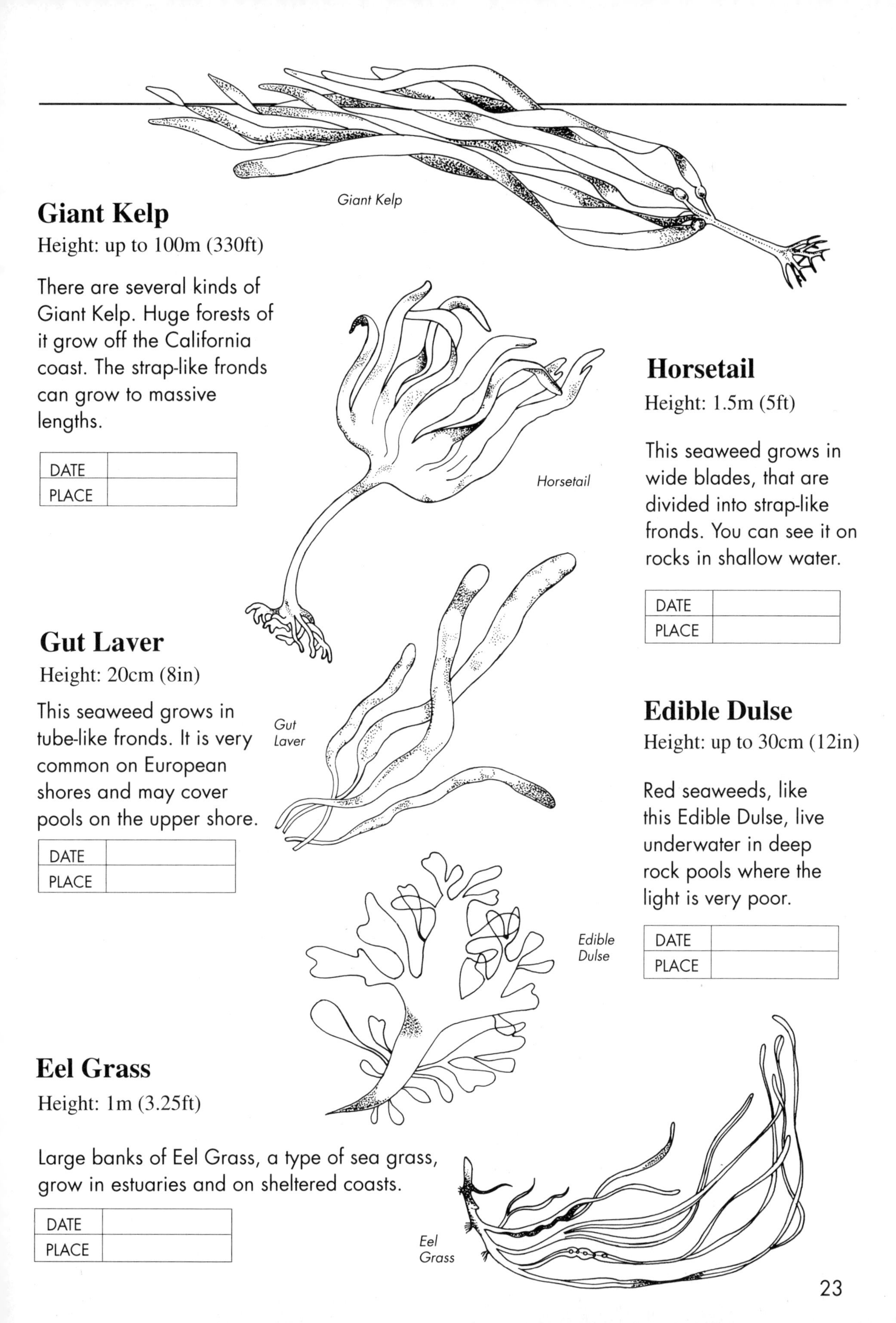

Giant Kelp

Height: up to 100m (330ft)

There are several kinds of Giant Kelp. Huge forests of it grow off the California coast. The strap-like fronds can grow to massive lengths.

DATE	
PLACE	

Horsetail

Height: 1.5m (5ft)

This seaweed grows in wide blades, that are divided into strap-like fronds. You can see it on rocks in shallow water.

DATE	
PLACE	

Gut Laver

Height: 20cm (8in)

This seaweed grows in tube-like fronds. It is very common on European shores and may cover pools on the upper shore.

DATE	
PLACE	

Edible Dulse

Height: up to 30cm (12in)

Red seaweeds, like this Edible Dulse, live underwater in deep rock pools where the light is very poor.

DATE	
PLACE	

Eel Grass

Height: 1m (3.25ft)

Large banks of Eel Grass, a type of sea grass, grow in estuaries and on sheltered coasts.

DATE	
PLACE	

INDEX AND CHECKLIST

This list will help you to find every seashore plant and animal in the book. The first number after each entry tells you which page it is on. The second number (in brackets) is the number of the sticker.

This book is based on material originally published in *Birdwatching, How Birds Live, Nature Trail Book of Seashore Life, Spotter's Guide to the Seashore, Spotter's Guide to Animals, Tracks and Signs, Spotter's Guide to Sea and Freshwater Birds, Spotter's Guide to Fishes* and *Nature Trail Book of Wild Flowers*. First published in 1997 by Usborne Publishing Ltd, Usborne House, 83-85 Saffron Hill, London, EC1N 8RT, England.

First published in America March 1998 AE

Printed in Italy.